THE ADVENTURES of the Rabbits in the Most Magical Place on Earth

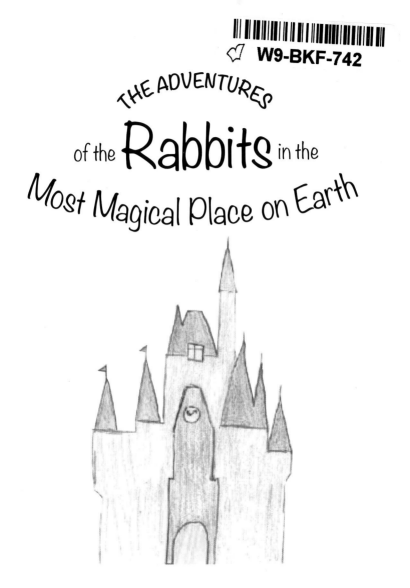

Written by **Austin Reich**   Illustrated by **Tyler Reich**

Printed in the United States of America

Cover and interior design by Susan Eugster

Library of Congress Control Number 2017906506
Photos on pages 52 and 53 used with permission ©Lifetouch Inc.

ISBN 978-0-9970808-8-9

2 4 6 8 10 9 7 5 3 1 paperback

Adventures of the
Real Animals in the
Most Magical Place on Earth

Visit our parent company at MommyMDGuides.com

To Mom and Dad

— **TYLER REICH**

To NaNa and PopPop

— **AUSTIN REICH**

Rebecca Rabbit woke with a yawn and a stretch. For a minute, she thought it was time to get up and get ready for school. Then she realized, it's summer vacation!

Rebecca looked around her family's nest. It was tidy and cozy, as all rabbits' nests are. A few feet away, Rebecca saw Mama Rabbit tidying up the fur that lined the nest. Just outside the nest, Rebecca saw Papa Rabbit picking some fresh grass for breakfast.

Rebecca and her family live
in a special place—the most magical
place on Earth, with a view of a beautiful
castle. But so far that morning, no
guests had arrived, the cleaning crews
had finished their work, and the rabbits,
squirrels, mice, and birds who make
their home in this magical place had
every inch of it to themselves.

"Time for breakfast," Papa Rabbit called.
Rebecca jumped out of her side of the nest,
nearly crashing into her brother, Eddie.

"Hey, watch out," Eddie grumbled,
never a morning rabbit, not even
on the first day of summer vacation.

"What have you two got planned
for today?" Mama Rabbit asked.

"I'm going to go play with Rachel,"
Rebecca said. Rachel Rabbit, Rebecca's cousin,
lived with her family just around the corner,
in a patch of grass near the 3D show.
(Rabbits can't read, so they don't know
the "real" names of any of the rides.)

Rebecca's Nest

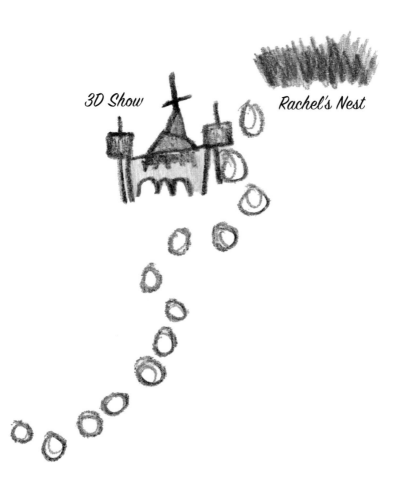

3D Show

Rachel's Nest

It was peaceful and quiet outside
the Rabbit family's nest. The air was warm,
but not yet hot. Rebecca could see the
spinning tea cups still, well, *still* for the night.

"Don't go any farther than the charging
stations," Mama Rabbit cautioned.
"It's not safe for you beyond there."

After a quick breakfast and a kiss from Mama,
Rebecca set off past the carousel.
She hopped past the dancing honey pots
with a nod to the family of mice
who live under the benches outside.

Rebecca stopped for a minute to admire herself in the reflection in a window of a shop.

Then out of the corner of her eye, she saw it—
a beautiful purple butterfly. Rebecca spun
around to get a closer look. It was the most
beautiful butterfly she had ever seen.
So Rebecca began to hop, hop, hop after the
butterfly. This was not an easy task because
butterflies do not fly in straight lines.
Rebecca hopped to the left, then to the right,
then to the left again, in pursuit
of the beautiful purple butterfly.

Rebecca was so busy hopping and watching the butterfly that she wasn't paying attention to where she was going. She never noticed when the bright colors of her home gave way to the red, white, and blue near the Liberty Bell.

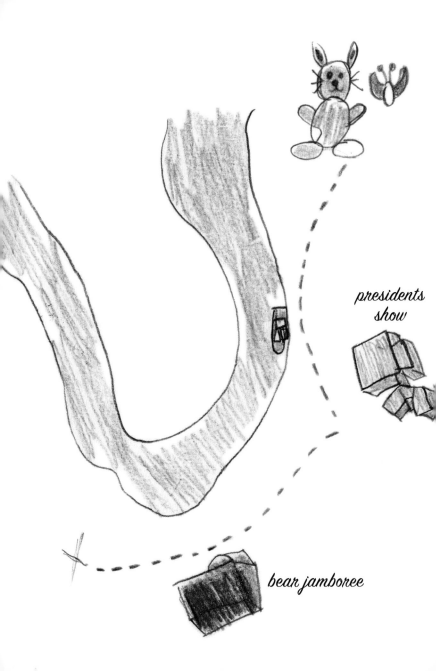

presidents
show

bear jamboree

Rebecca hopped right past the
presidents show without blinking an eye.
She followed the butterfly right past
the bear jamboree too.

Suddenly, the butterfly landed on a bush near a curvy path. Rebecca stopped for a moment to look and listen. She was shocked and frightened to realize that she didn't know where she was. What are those giant flying carpets overhead? What is that building with the thatched roof and the birds sitting outside? Where is that sound of the beating drums coming from?

Rebecca didn't realize it, but she had wandered far from her home and was now in a tropical land. Completely lost and more than a little bit scared, Rebecca found a bench and huddled beneath it. She didn't know what to do, so she thought she'd rest for a bit.

Having hopped so far already that morning, soon Rebecca fell asleep in the cool shade underneath the bench.

But as the time passed, back at the Rabbit's nest, Mama Rabbit and Papa Rabbit began to worry that Rebecca hadn't come home. Soon hours had gone by.

"Where could she be?"
Papa Rabbit asked Mama Rabbit.
He had already searched all around the
carousel, the singing doll boatride,
and the flying boatride, looking
for Rebecca in her usual places.

"I don't know," Mama Rabbit replied.
"I think we need to get help to go look for her."

Papa Rabbit hopped out of the nest to a tree
nearby where a family of swallows lived.

"Will you help me find my daughter, Rebecca?"
Papa Rabbit asked.

"Of course," answered the swallows.
The birds flew high above the most magical place
on Earth, searching for Rebecca. They swirled
above the dancing honey pots, the castle,
the slow-moving blue train, the ice cream parlor,
the haunted house, and finally near the very
cheerful singing bird ride. It was there that
they spotted Rebecca, huddled beneath
the bench in the unfamiliar tropical land.

"Rebecca, Rebecca," the swallows cried.
"Your family is worried about you.
Are you okay?"

"Yes," Rebecca answered, trembling.
"Follow us," the swallows called.
"We'll guide you home."

Rebecca hopped as fast as she could,
following the swallows back past the flying
carpets, past the shooting gallery, past the tall,
skinny tower, and safely back to her home.
Just as Rebecca made it back to the nest,
the skies opened up, and it began to rain.

"Thank you," Rebecca called to the swallows.
"I'm so very glad to be home,"
she said to her family.

The rain made a soft soothing
sound on the rabbit's nest
as the family settled in for the night.

"I love a rainy night," said Rebecca's brother,
Eddie, peering up at the night sky.
The whole Rabbit family was happy
that Rebecca was home safe and sound.

Tyler's Top Travel Tips

Tyler is an 11-year-old sixth grader. He's been to the most magical place on Earth six times! Tyler's favorite thing to do there is shop at the LEGO store.

Here are Tyler's top travel tips.

- It's fun to sit down with your family a few months ahead of your trip and choose the restaurants you want to eat at. In my family, we each choose one special meal for our trip.

- Also, a few months ahead of time, you could sit down together and pick the rides you most want to ride. When I go to with my mom and brother, we each choose one favorite ride per day.

- Before you go, you can decorate envelopes in which your parents can put tips for the housekeepers at the resort.

- When you choose your bands, you might want to each pick different colors so you can easily tell them apart—although they do print your name also on the inside. Or you could do what my family does and all get the same color so you match.

- Consider bringing a poncho from home. They cost around $9 in the parks.

- Several attractions in the parks have height requirements. Ask your parents to measure you, wearing the shoes you'll wear on your trip. Google "attraction height requirements" so you know ahead of time if, for example, you won't be able to ride a particular attraction.

- You can get your hair cut at the barber shop on Main Street. They can put in colored hair gel too.

- You can join in a pirate's adventure. This interactive quest is free, and you get a free map and talisman to keep. It starts at the Crow's Nest, which is near the Pirates ride.

- Look for the wishing well. If you toss in some of your change, you can make a wish and know that your change will be donated to charity.

- Want to get a high score on the Buzz ride? Keep the trigger depressed the entire time.

- At the speedway, ask for a free driver's license!

- In the Figment ride, in the smell lab, look at the pipes and tanks. There are some funny jokes printed on them. Take some time to play after riding the Figment ride in the Imageworks Labs.

- You can design your own virtual car and then ride it on the race car ride. After the ride, you can create a 15-second commercial for your car and email it to your friends and family.

- There aren't many attractions at World Showcase, so you might want to pick up a F.O.N.E. (Field Operative Notification Equipment) from a kiosk near Norway, Italy, or United Kingdom and play the Phineas and Ferb: Agent P's World Showcase Adventure. You solve puzzles and clues in this interactive adventure. You don't get to keep the F.O.N.E, but the game is fun. You'll mind less if your parents want to wander into every single store in World Showcase.

Austin's Top Travel Tips

Austin is a 9-year-old fourth grader. He has also been to the most magical place on Earth six times! Austin's favorite thing to do there is to swim in the resort pools and water parks, especially the wave pool.

Here are Austin's top travel tips.

- It's fun to trade pins with cast members. You can tell who's a cast member because they all wear oval name tags.

- Check out the cast members' hometowns, which are also listed on their nametags. Maybe you'll meet someone from your own town.

- A fun, and free, thing to do either on your first night or for a break is to ride the monorails. The world has 14.7 miles of monorail track. There are three monorail loops.

- If you're going to spend your money on a misting fan, buy it on the first day of your trip, so you can enjoy it your whole trip.

- In all of the parks, you'll see some cast members wearing photographer clothing. These are park photographers, and they are staked out at the best photo spots. Your parents can buy these special photos, but if you ask, the cast members will also be happy to take your family photo with your camera.

- In addition to hunting for characters (see page 49 for our favorites), you can look for survey markers. They are small metal disks in the ground that say "Survey Markers" on them.

- If you get scared while waiting in line for an attraction, like the haunted house, let your parents and a cast member know. They can let you out a "hidden" exit.

- At the kingdom, there's a free interactive game called Sorcerers of the Magic Kingdom. The premise of the game is that the villains are trying to take over the park. To learn how to play—and to get a free pack of Sorcerers of the Magic Kingdom trading cards and beautiful map—stop by the firehouse on Main Street, U.S.A. A cast member will teach you how to play the game, which you can play as little or as much as you want in the park.

- If it's super hot, super cold, super crowded, or raining, you can stay out of the weather on Main Street, U.S.A. by walking through the stores. They're all inter-connected.

- You can get really soaked on the flume ride. If you want to stay drier, sit on the left side of the log. Or wear your poncho!

- You can take the Friendship Boats across the lagoon to the countries, rather than trekking the long way around.

- In the countries, pick up a Duffy on a stick at any Kidcot Fun Stop. You can color it there or take it home. The cast members at each county pavilion then can stamp the stick.

- A great place to eat lunch is the Katsura Grill in Japan. Be sure to stop in the store too; they sell lots of great things, including Cat O Lucks.

- There's a little play area for little kids outside the Seas with Nemo & Friends attraction. It's called Bruce's Shark World, and it has some hands-on activities.

- Nearby, you'll see a huge manmade Caribbean coral reef. If you get there early, you'll get to see them feeding the fish.

- Do you like soda? You can drink all of the free soda you want—well, at least all of the free soda your parents will let you drink—at Club Cool. You can try eight Coca-Cola sodas from around the world. You can even take one of the tiny cups home as a free souvenir.

- If you have time, it's fun to ride safaris a second time on the same day. It will be a very different experience, and you'll probably see different animals. The animals are often livelier later in the day too.

- Want a fun souvenir? By the Oasis Bridge look for the W.E. Headquarters. That's for Wilderness Explorer, from the movie *UP*. After taking the pledge, you get a free field guide. Scattered around the park are about 30 different challenges to complete and earn badges.

- In the afternoon, it's fun to spend a few hours in the "play area." This gives your parents a little break too! You can walk from the climbing/sliding area across the bridge to the dig area. Let your parents know you're doing that before you cross though!

- If you like animals, you can see another entire savannah at the resort. Even if you're not staying there, you can go to look. There are many viewing areas throughout the resort, including a four-story observation window in the lobby. Be sure to go during the day because there are no lights on the savannah.

TYLER AND AUSTIN'S
Favorite Hidden Characters

Throughout the parks, the designers have hid their favorite character's shape like little Easter eggs for us to find. The classic hidden character is the three circles, but you might also find his profile, and even the occasional other character. Can you find these hidden characters, using our clues?

You'll need to take a boat ride to pet some animals to see this on a huge mural.

On a boat rode through gardens, can you find this tree?

Visit a sandy place and look on a fence for this familiar sight.

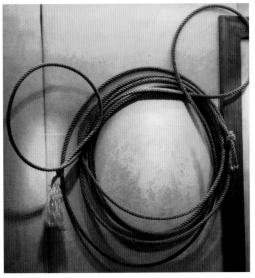

While shopping in a frontier trading post, look behind the counter!

In the animal themed resort, look up!

In the same boat ride through the beautiful gardens, can you spot this familiar figure?

ABOUT THE ILLUSTRATOR

Tyler is an 11-year-old sixth grader. He loves drawing, traveling, playing with his friends, LEGO, and Pokémon.

ABOUT THE WRITER

Austin is a nine-year-old fourth grader. He loves reading, traveling, playing with his friends, LEGO, and Pokémon.

Our Partners!

Many thanks to our partners
for their encouragement
and support.

Want to partner with us?

Email:
jenniferreich@mommymdguides.com

We have lots of great ideas
to join forces.

Jennifer, Tyler, and Austin Reich

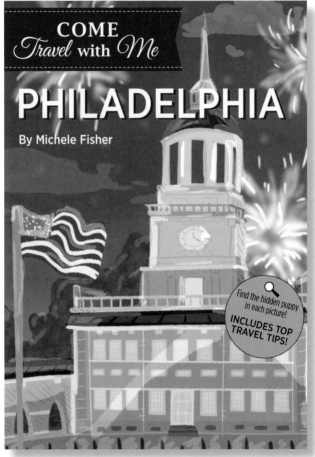

The Mommy MD Guides™

Motherhood is a journey.
Mommy MDs are your guides.
www.MommyMDGuides.com

● **Order our books online at many sites, including Walmart.com, Amazon.com, and MommyMDGuides.com**

● **Purchase them at bookstores nationwide**

● **Download them for your Kindle, Nook, or iPhone/iPad**

● ● ● ● ● ● ● ● ●

Enjoy more Mommy MD Guides' tips on

The Mommy MD Guide to Pregnancy and Birth app.

Visit us at MommyMDGuides.com
and DaddyMDGuides.com.

COMING SOON!

*The Mommy MD Guides are hard at work on more titles in the series.
Keep a lookout for:*

The Mommy MD Guide to Keeping Your Baby Safe

Coming in Fall 2017

EVERYWHERE BOOKS ARE SOLD

Adventures of the
Real Animals in the
Most Magical Place on Earth

Tyler and Austin are hard at work
at more books in their
Adventures of the Real Animals
in the Most Magical Place on Earth series.
(Can you say "Research Trip!"?)

Watch for these titles, coming soon
from Momosa Publishing LLC

· *The Adventures of the Squirrels in the Most Magical Place in Earth*

· *The Adventures of the Lions in the Most Magical Place in Earth*

· *The Adventures of the Geckos in the Most Magical Place in Earth*

· *The Adventures of the Frogs the Most Magical Place in Earth*

Available everywhere books are sold!

Buy our books online!
Order them in stores!
Ask for them at your library!

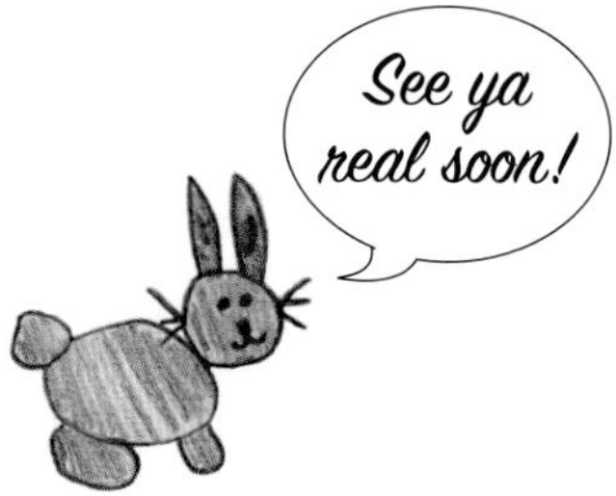
See ya
real soon!